The Pea Patch Jig
Thacher Hurd

Creston Books

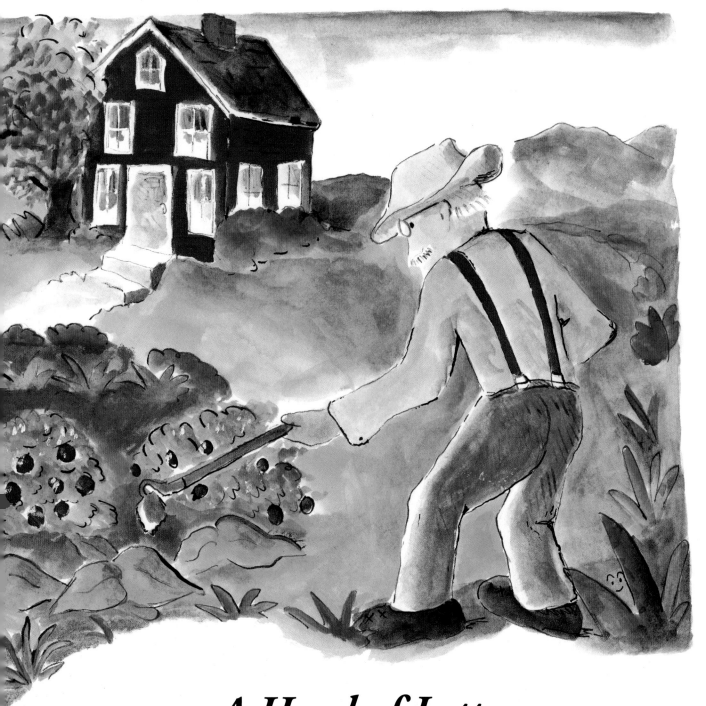

A Head of Lettuce

Where the pole beans climb, where the tomatoes grow fat, where the onions smell sweet, and the corn is yellow as the summer sun, that's the garden of Clem — Farmer Clem. All day long Farmer Clem worked in the garden, hoeing, raking, and weeding.

Farmer Clem was so busy gardening that he didn't see
the tiny family that lived at the edge of the garden:
Father Mouse, Mother Mouse, and Baby Mouse.

Clem's garden was their garden too, though Farmer Clem
didn't know it.

One day, while Mother and Father Mouse were busy with
the preparations for their midsummer party, Baby Mouse
wandered away.

Baby Mouse walked past the beets, corn, onions, and parsley. She came to the lettuce. Baby mouse was tired. She was ready for her nap.

Baby Mouse climbed into a head of lettuce.

Mother called out, "BABY, WHERE ARE YOU?" Baby
didn't answer. Father yelled, "BABY, COME HOME!"
Baby didn't answer. Baby was fast asleep.

Meanwhile, Farmer Clem came out of his house to gather vegetables for his dinner. He picked tomatoes, he picked carrots, he picked a big zucchini, *AND...*

he picked the head of lettuce in
which Baby Mouse lay fast asleep.

Mother and Father Mouse soon discovered the disaster.
They looked through Farmer Clem's kitchen window.

He was making a salad.
A SALAD?!!!
Father Mouse ran to the top kitchen shelf and peered over
the big zucchini. Mother Mouse stayed behind the tomato.
Clem put the head of lettuce on the cutting board. He took
out his knife. He raised his knife.

Father Mouse yelled, "TIMBERRRRR!" as he pushed the big zucchini off the shelf. *THWACK!!!* It landed on Farmer Clem's head.

Father Mouse fell down the back of Clem's shirt. "JAKERS CRAKERS!" cried Clem.

Mother reached deep into the lettuce. There was Baby, still asleep. Father Mouse fell out of Clem's shirt. He ran past the dishwasher. He ran past the blender. Father Mouse, Mother Mouse, and Baby Mouse jumped out the window,

into Clem's compost heap. *SQUISH!*
"JAKERS CRAKERS!" said Father Mouse.
He pulled Mother Mouse and Baby Mouse out of the potato peelings and stale bread, and the Mouse family ran home as fast as they could.

The Big Tomato

After such a big adventure, Mother decided that Baby should have a bath. She filled the bathtub up with warm, soapy water and put Baby in. Then she went off to finish her last-minute preparations for the party.

Baby looked around the bathtub. There was nothing to play with. Baby wanted a ball. Baby climbed out of the bathtub and walked out the back door, back into Clem's garden.

Baby walked past the beets, corn, onions, parsley, and lettuce. Baby came to the tomatoes. She looked up at them. They looked like balls hanging from a tree.

Baby climbed up a tomato plant and kicked one off.
SPLAT!!! Baby thought that was fun.

Baby forgot about her bath. Baby sat in the tomato plant,
kicking off tomatoes.

The guests were starting to arrive for the party. They were all dressed up. Grandfather and Grandmother Mouse were making their way through the vegetable garden. They walked under the tomato plant.

SPLAT! A tomato was stuck on Grandfather's head. "MMMMMPPPPHHHHH!" Grandfather hopped around the garden.

Father and Mother came out. "BABY!" they cried, when they saw Baby in the tomato plant and Grandfather with his head in a tomato. Now it was Grandfather who needed a bath.

A Mess of Peas

Soon all the guests had arrived. Everyone was in a jolly mood. They were sitting on the front porch, shucking peas and looking at Baby. "What a cute baby," they all said. Mother was finishing dinner. Last of all she cooked the peas.

Then everyone gathered around the table and sat down to dinner. Baby sat in her high chair, eating peas with her fingers and drinking milk through a straw.

After dinner Baby went upstairs and fed her teddy bear peas and milk through a straw. Then Mother tucked Baby in bed and kissed her good night.

Baby couldn't get to sleep. Baby looked out the window. The moon was full. Everyone was out in the garden, talking.

Baby took out her straw and started to shoot leftover peas with it. "OUCH!" said Grandfather. "OUCH!!" said Grandmother. "Darn mosquitoes!!!" said Father. No one saw Baby shooting peas in the dark.

Then Baby saw something no one else saw. Something creeping through the lettuce on tiptoe. Something with red fur and sharp teeth, hungry for a little morsel of mouse... *PTTTOOOOOOIIIIIII!!!* Baby shot a pea.

YEEEEOOOOWWW!!! It jumped. A FOX! Everyone ran inside. They leaned out the window and yelled at the fox. They yelled so loudly, they woke up Farmer Clem. Farmer Clem ran out to the vegetable garden.

But all he saw was the fox's bushy red tail disappearing across the meadow. Farmer Clem went back to bed. Soon he was snoring as loudly as before.

Everyone went back outside. Grandfather brought out his fiddle and tuned it up. Mother brought costumes out of the family trunk.

Soon everyone was dressed up as vegetables. They made a circle in the middle of the garden and Grandfather started to play "The Pea Patch Jig." Everyone danced beneath the midsummer moon.

Baby wanted to be a vegetable too — a bright green pea. And she wanted to dance where the pole beans climb, where the tomatoes grow fat, where the onions smell sweet, and the corn is as yellow as the summer sun.

"The Pea Patch Jig" can be found on the album
Vassar Clements, John Hartford, Dave Holland (vinyl and cassette)
or streaming online at crestonbooks.co.

Very special thanks to John Hartford for his discovery, arrangement,
and musical autography of "The Pea Patch Jig" by Dan Emmett.
Copyright © 1986 by John Hartford Music, B.M.I.
Reprinted by permission.

CIP data for this book is available from the Library of Congress.

Published by Creston Books, LLC
www.crestonbooks.co

Source of Production: Worzalla Books, Stevens Point, Wisconsin
Printed and bound in the United States of America
Illustrations composed of watercolor on paper.
Type set in Caslon Pro, Garamond, and Kreon.
1 2 3 4 5